Let Them **Eat Cake!**

By Frank Berrios
Illustrated by Fabio Laguna and James Gallego

A Random House PICTUREBACK® Book

Random House 🏠 New York

"Mr. Peabody & Sherman" © 2014 DreamWorks Animation L.L.C. Character rights TM & © Ward Productions, Inc. Licensed by Bullwinkle Studios, LLC. All rights reserved. Published in the United States by Random House Children's Books, a division of Random House LLC, 1745 Broadway, New York, NY 10019, and in Canada by Random House of Canada Limited, Toronto, Penguin Random House Companies. Pictureback, Random House, and the Random House colophon are registered trademarks of Random House LLC.
randomhouse.com/kids
ISBN 978-0-385-37147-6
Printed in the United States of America
10 9 8 7 6 5 4 3 2 1

Mr. Peabody was a dog, but he was also a scientist, an Olympic gold medalist, a chef, and possibly the world's smartest individual.

To teach his boy, Sherman, all about history, Mr. Peabody created a time-traveling machine called the **WABAC** (pronounced "way back"). On their latest adventure, they used the WABAC to travel back in time and attend a party given by Marie Antoinette, Queen of France!

"Introducing the most honored and honorable Mr. Peabody and his boy, Sherman!" announced the royal servant.

After a quick dance with the queen, Mr. Peabody introduced her to Sherman.

"Hi, Ms. Antoinette," said Sherman. "May I have some cake?"

Delighted, Marie Antoinette replied,
"Let zem eat cake!"

Unfortunately, two starving peasants overheard the queen. They scurried off to tell the other peasants what they thought they had heard.

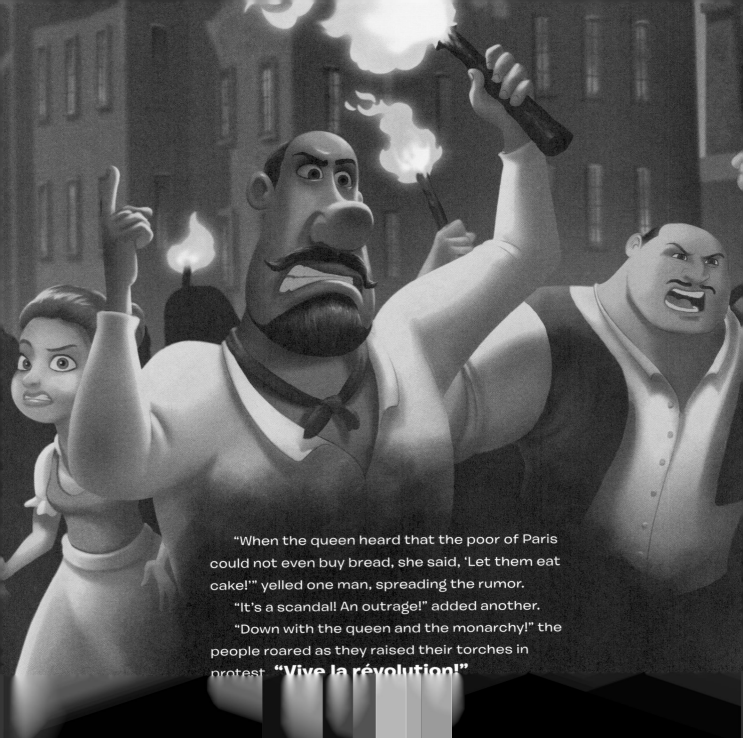

"When the queen heard that the poor of Paris could not even buy bread, she said, 'Let them eat cake!'" yelled one man, spreading the rumor.

"It's a scandal! An outrage!" added another.

"Down with the queen and the monarchy!" the people roared as they raised their torches in protest. **"Vive la révolution!"**

Crash! When a brick flew through a window, Mr. Peabody knew it was time to leave. After bidding farewell to the queen, he found that Sherman had wandered off.

Mr. Peabody found Sherman
munching on cake in the kitchen.

"Sherman, don't you remember why I told you
to stay close to me during the French Revolution?"

"Because after the French Revolution,
it's gonna rain?" answered Sherman.

"Close. I said, 'After the French Revolution comes the **Reign of Terror!**'" replied Mr. Peabody just as a mob of angry peasants stormed in.
"Round up the aristocrats!" they yelled, pointing to Mr. Peabody.

Mr. Peabody was hauled off to the public square. The mob was shouting, **"Punish him!"**

Things looked grim for Mr. Peabody as Sherman forced his way to the front of the crowd.

"Mr. Peabody, what should I do?" yelled Sherman.

"Nothing, Sherman!" said Mr. Peabody. "Everything's going to be fine. Just stay right there!"

"Off with his head!" ordered Robespierre, one of the leaders of the revolution.

The blade of the guillotine dropped. Robespierre reached down for Mr. Peabody's head—and was shocked to find a cantaloupe instead! Mr. Peabody had escaped! **"Get that dog!"** he yelled.

"Mr. Peabody, how'd you escape?" asked Sherman as they ran through the sewer.

"Simple, really," replied Mr. Peabody. "I noticed the sewer lid beneath the guillotine platform, noted the loose board under the basket, and swiped the executioner's melon to give me the added weight to tip the board so I could make my exit."

Suddenly, Robespierre appeared
in front of them with his troops.
"Aha! I've got you now!" he cried.
"All right, Sherman, looks like it's
time for a little pop quiz in the art of
fencing," said Mr. Peabody, preparing
to fight.

Sherman cried out,
**"Attack!
Parry!
   Thrust!
Remise!"**

Robespierre was a talented swordsman, but he was no
match for Mr. Peabody. Before long, Mr. Peabody had disarmed
and defeated his foe—but Robespierre's troops were still
ready to battle.

Mr. Peabody tossed his sword at the remaining troops. The sword missed everyone but pierced the pipe behind them.

"Ha, ha—you missed!" they taunted him.

"I never miss," replied Mr. Peabody as water began to trickle out of the pipe.

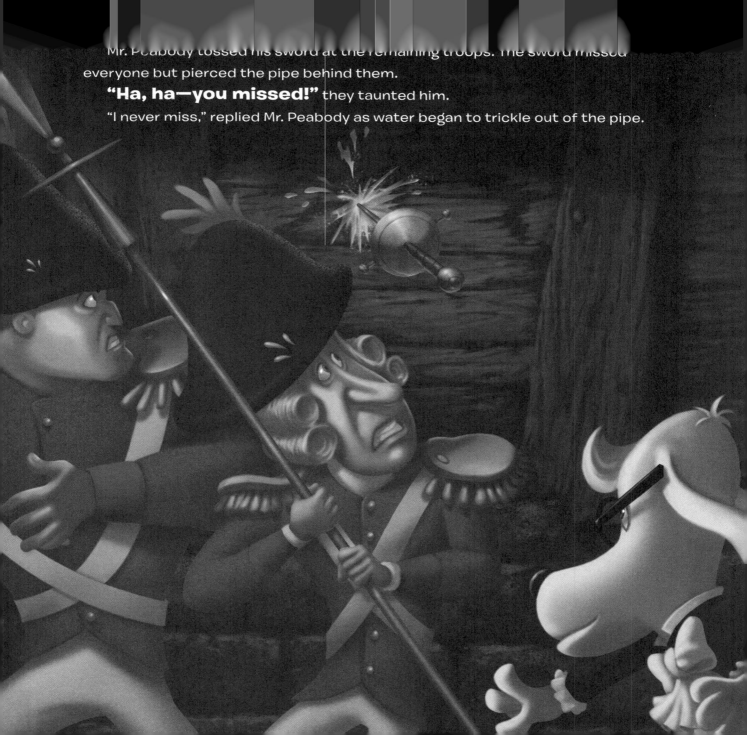

Suddenly, the pipe burst—sending a wave of water racing through the sewer!

"Hop on!" said Mr. Peabody, using a sewer cap to surf the wave. "Do you smell that, Sherman?"

"It wasn't me, Mr. Peabody," replied Sherman.

"I know it wasn't you. It's the methane gas in the sewer system. And we're about to use it to blast out of here! **Hang on!**"

Mr. Peabody scraped the wall with the metal sewer cap, causing sparks, which ignited the gas, and . . .

KABOOM!

"Wow!" said Sherman as they blasted out of the sewer and into the sky.

They rode the sewer cap like a snowboard down a tall tree and landed safely on the ground.

"So, what did we learn today?" asked Mr. Peabody.

"That the French Revolution was **crazy!** When Mrs. Antoinette said 'Let them eat cake,' she wasn't talking about the poor—she was talking about us!" replied Sherman.

"Yes, the history we find in books and films is often filled with misunderstandings, half-truths, and sometimes downright lies. That's why I built you the **WABAC**," said Mr. Peabody.

"Where are we gonna go tomorrow?" asked Sherman. "Ancient Rome? The Wild West?"

"No, Sherman. Tomorrow's adventure is one that you're going to be taking all on your own," replied Mr. Peabody. **"It's your first day at school."**